STICKS & and STONES

CHICKEN HOUSE PRESS

Sticks & Stones

Copyright © 2025 by Chicken House Press

This book is a collection of literary works by Canadians. Copyright of each piece herein belongs to the individual author.

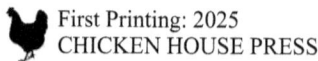 First Printing: 2025
CHICKEN HOUSE PRESS

Print ISBN: 978-1-990336-90-4

Chicken House Press
282906 Normanby/Bentinck Townline
Durham, Ontario, Canada, N0G 1R0
www.chickenhousepress.ca

Contact the publisher for Library and Archives Canada catalogue information.

Chicken House Press acknowledges the support of *Blank Spaces* Magazine for sponsorship of the writing content that culminated in these final eight stories.

Thanks is also due to the judging panel who selected these eight stories to be included: Anne Baldo, Gary Kirchner, Michelle McLaughlin, Joanne Morrison, Sorche Patterson, and Alanna Rusnak.

Hamlet by William Shakespeare (1564-1616) Originally published by Andrew Wise in 1597 (public domain)

Cover design by Alanna Rusnak

Though this be madness, yet there is method in't.

William Shakespeare

CONTENTS

FOREWORD

Sticks and stones may break my bones.
But words will never hurt me.

"Sticks and Stones" is a provocative theme for a short story collection. The phrase is drawn from a reassuring adage for children being teased or bullied: primal weaponry is juxtaposed against language to empower the victim, who is reminded that verbal taunts cannot physically wound them. Words leave no visible marks or scars, so they cannot hurt.

When this defiant chant was first used in the mid nineteenth-century, the invisible psychological trauma caused by verbal abuse was not understood. Insults were evanescent and impermanent and so could be dismissed. At the same time, physical violence was often a part of daily life—corporal punishment was routinely used to discipline children, and bullying was considered a standard rite of passage. In that context, insulting language would be the lesser pain.

In the 21st century, however, we know more about the long-term effects of emotional abuse and how memories of harsh language can revive trauma. The psychic damage caused by verbal taunts can be permanently damaging. For better or worse, words can and do hurt—because words matter. That they linger in the mind and keep on hurting is evidence of the power of language.

Of course, words do much more than abuse or control, just as sticks and stones are more than just weapons. Language makes the world even when the body and its vulnerable bones are not at stake. In this collection, words capture the variegated challenges of existence and draw us into eight different worlds made of words that linger. The image of "sticks and stones" is at the core of all of them, with each becoming a meditation on how to navigate the awkward tensions between the mind and the body, between emotional pain and somatic suffering and, ultimately, between abstract representation and physical reality.

The stories in this collection challenge the imperviousness of language implied by the original adage. All written narratives do—words are key to common understanding, and in fiction can be used to draw us into the experiences of others. We can see how words can both break the spirit and also revive it. Offering thoughtful and sometimes oblique perspectives on the schoolyard retort, each of these stories draws upon and creates a common ground that goes beyond the simple materiality implied by sticks and stones.

The opening story, Cornelia Mars's *Sticks and Stones*, addresses the collection's themes most literally, using an act of violent bullying to explore the confusion of childhood. A young Canadian girl, trying to adapt to life in a foreign country after her father disappears, finds herself confronted by a group of boys who attack her with sticks and stones. She successfully escapes and in the process discovers her resilience.

And Three More, by Rose Camara, takes the reader step by step through a therapy session in which the narrator confronts a deeply blocked memory. Seeking to overcome feelings of guilt associated with her sibling's death, she traverses mental obstacles and tortured recollections, each of which is presented as a static destination, in order to reach the final site of the original traumatizing event. Her emotional state at the end is open, but the recovery of the long-buried memory suggests a new journey of recovery lies ahead.

In Tara Ross's *Hatchling,* a mother planning to leave her family is preparing dinner when her children discover a nest of turtle hatchlings being threatened by crows. Detailed descriptions of domestic activity are juxtaposed against the narrator's conflicting thoughts on maternal responsibility and her desire for freedom. The violence of the natural world prompts her to consider the damage her impending departure will inflict on her family.

The Scavenger's Garden, by Nikki Berreth, presents a shift in tone away from the intimate emotional realism of the first three stories. In this work of speculative fiction, a young girl defies her parents' expectations in order to forge a new path for herself. In this futuristic world, everyone is assigned a role predetermined by family tradition and history—and she has been born into a stoneworker family. In an act of quiet rebellion, she creates a secret vegetable garden that grows in tandem with her maturation.

In Katrine Raymond's beautifully detailed *Keepsakes,* main character Jimmy discovers new information about his family while cleaning out his dead mother's house. He processes his grief by reading the personal notes his mother has taped to her possessions; as he learns about more her past and his own, he must face an altered sense of self and of family.

A young woman confronts her guilt about her treatment of a friend who has died in the darkly witty *Bones,* by E. J. Nash. The narrator's cruel words have ended a close friendship, and she is haunted by the memory, which takes the form of a talking skeleton that hides in her closet. She is simultaneously repulsed and fascinated by this palpable manifestation of her guilt, even as it forces her to confront her toxic behaviour.

In Andrea Marcelino's fantastical *Slippery Silver,* a young poet longing for motherhood finds herself invited to a series of mysterious parties populated by artistic eccentrics. An unexpected experience at one of these events concludes with an evocative and hopeful dream of fulfillment.

The final tale, *Ovomancy,* by K. R. Wilson, is a carefully wrought exploration of wounded masculinity. An anxious middle-aged man finds an unexpected prophecy fulfilled when he suffers a humiliating fall in front of other men. The creative use of egg imagery augments the protagonist's struggles with male fragility and potency. Told in the future tense, the story reads like a prophecy as it considers the extent to which life is controllable and self-knowledge possible.

E. Yvonne Pelletier

former Professor of Women's Studies and Senior Lecturer on British and American Literature of the 19th Century, grand prize judge of the *Blank Spaces*/Chicken House Press Anthology Contest

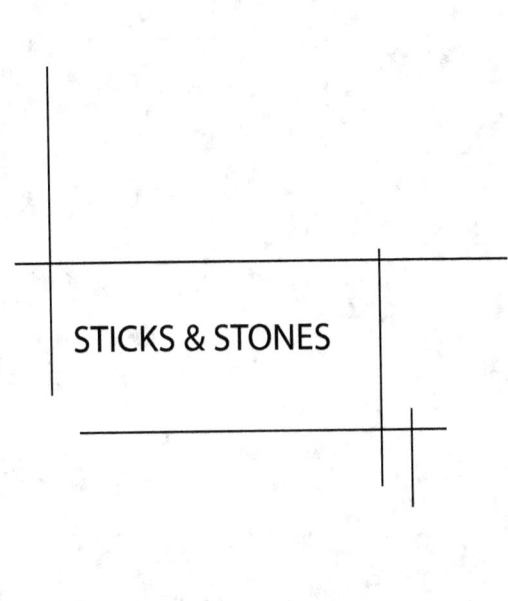

STICKS & STONES

STICKS AND STONES

Cornelia Mars

I started first grade about a month after Dad disappeared. This would have been in 1986, the year I turned 7. I don't recall the exact time frame, but I remember that he left in summer while my sister, Mom, and I were on holiday in Canada. That's where we had lived before moving to Sweden. When we returned to our apartment by the train tracks, five stops north of Stockholm, we were greeted by extra closet space and a bowl of rotting peaches. I haven't retained much after the peaches, except for how my sister and I watched TV while Mom dialled her way through the address book. I do remember understanding that he had gone and that nobody knew where he was, but everything after that is pretty much blank. I don't recall crying or waiting by the door (although I imagine I must have done both because I was a child quick to tears and tantrums). I don't remember going to get my baby brother at our grandparents, or preparing for school. I don't remember getting a backpack or Mom pinning up my bangs with those plastic barrettes that were impossible to adjust without ripping your hair out. I don't even remember that first walk up the hill to the yellow brick building where the neighbourhood kids attended elementary. I don't recall feeling one way or another about it. At some point, however, my memory flicked back on, and by that time, I was already well into the alphabet.

I remember sitting at my desk filling up a page in my exercise book with big letter Es. I took special care to connect the dots on the guideline to make the middle stroke, and when I wavered even a little, I erased my mistakes and did it over again. Sofia sat on my left and Malin behind me, to the right. The three of us kept close track of each other's progress, competing for praise, but I could rarely catch up because I tried too hard. By the end of the day my desk was covered in eraser crumbs. Our teacher, Eva, didn't seem to mind. She had choppy grey hair, spindly arms, and might have looked scary to a 7-year-old if she hadn't been so kind. I adored her for her patience—the kind Mom had very little of —but also because she knew all about our situation.

At some point, before the first snowfall, Mom had come to my school for a parent-teacher meeting. The way I remember it, she was late. Her fur coat—beaver, from Canada—swayed as she rushed down the hall. After the perfunctory progress report, Mom and Eva chatted in the hallway. Even though I couldn't hear everything they were saying, I knew Mom was explaining the circumstances of Dad's disappearance because of the hushed voices and how she repeated the word "he" over and over. (That's what Mom called Dad after he left.) As she spoke, Mom twirled the air with her vermillion-tipped fingers, as if undoing a magic spell. After that, Eva and I had a special connection. She had lost someone close too. This is what Mom told me afterwards.

I don't know what our routine was like for Mom, now that she was alone with three kids, working full-time and overtime to boot, but I distill something from the fact that I don't remember her ever sitting down. Her face seemed perpetually obscured by movement. Her hair curtained around her features as she bent to zip up a coat or pick up a stray Garbage Pail Kids card. While we ate dinner, she was always running down to the basement to do laundry. I try to recall the mornings but can't, not in images. The thing that remains is the sound of our voices echoing down the spiral stairwell of our apartment block as we waited for the jangle of the elevator. If I reach deeper, I can almost see the end of our street (always gravelly in my memory) and Mom's coat flapping open because she never had time to button anything up for herself. But this may just be how I pieced things together in retrospect—after I became a mother—the way you measure a black hole, not by any visible presence, but by how light behaves around it.

My siblings and I never spoke about Dad disappearing

but we all knew what had been going on. The sounds of their fights had pushed into our bedroom, much like the smoke from Mom's Yellow Blend cigarettes, or the newscasts about Chernobyl, which reminded us that there were poisons in this world that could creep up on you, needle into your bones, and kill you without so much as casting a shadow.

At some point that winter, new anxieties sprouted up in the murkiness of my being, like puffball mushrooms on a forest trail. Along with the typical kid rituals of not stepping on cracks, I developed a few other habits. If I bumped myself, I had to slap or pinch the equivalent place on the opposite side of my body. I was also a compulsive chewer and bit down on my pencils in neat patterns, slowly, so I could feel the paint crack. If I think about those pencils, my memory starts to sharpen. All kinds of details unfurl from that: by the end of a lesson I often had flecks of yellow around my lips and the sweet taste of cedar in my mouth. Although I tried hard not to chew off the eraser heads, I often couldn't help myself, any more than I could stop playing with the rash in the fold of my left earlobe.

In some ways, I was still the fearless tomboy I had always been—unfazed by (and even drawn to) things like climbing tall trees and riding rollercoasters—but I was getting nervous about other things, like whether we could afford groceries. Then, at some point, my longing for Dad pivoted to a gnawing fear of losing Mom. I worried about her getting cancer from smoking too many Yellow Blends. I worried about her heels on the ice and how the long-distance trains whipped the air around you on the platform when they passed. But the thing I worried about most was psycho killers busting into our apartment. The only way I could think to communicate this was to ask Mom if she had locked the door. When she said "Yes" (which she always did) I would ask her to double check. I could only relax once I heard the thud of the bolt and the click of the stainless steel cup that protected the lock in case someone slipped a jimmy through the mail shoot. Mom always humoured me and checked. She'd pat my head. If that wasn't enough, she would illustrate what she would do if anyone tried any nonsense by grabbing the fox pelt we had found in the storage cage in the basement and swinging it by its tail until it was horizontal. Then she'd let go and let it fly. Whoosh, gone. I didn't realize until much later that perhaps she had been just as scared as me. One day, more than twenty years later, she did describe how she had looked over her shoulder for years, scared that Dad would appear out of the shadows and do good on his threat to kill her.

At the end of my school day, I would cross the street and go to a home daycare, with a lady named Anna-Lena who lived in a low-rise with yellow stucco walls. This quiet neighbourhood where I spent most of my time was only a fifteen minute walk from where we lived, but my memories of that area—the glossy school desks, monthly visits from the fluoride lady, and Anna-Lena with her oat cookies and bottles of perm solution—have a different hue than the ones I have of our home, which are still obscured by the rush of long-distance trains and wilful amnesia.

I do have one memory of my two worlds intersecting when one day, Markus, a boy in my class with a crew cut and flipped bangs like Dennis the Menace, confronted me in the hallway.

"Hey, uh, where's your dad?" he said as if he'd given the question some thought and had to muster up the courage to ask it. I wanted to tell him that I'd like to know the answer to that myself, but I knew no one was going to give it to me.

"How should I know?" I said, eyeballing him.

"But, but..." Markus hesitated and looked around at the others who had gathered behind him. He was confused by my flippant answer—as if I didn't care, which is what I wanted him to think—and also by the fact that I didn't know. Even the kids with divorced parents knew where their dads were. There would be some kind of gesture to go with the whereabouts of a dad, something in the vein of how the balding weatherman on *Rapport* announced a low pressure with possible showers, with a lifted arm, an index sweeping sideways: over there. Plus, everyone knew that dads came and went like clockwork. Out at six back at sixteen hundred. That's how it was with his dad, Stefan's dad, and even Sofia's dad, and he wasn't Swedish any more than my dad was. Suddenly I felt ashamed in a brand new way, all the way into the pit of my stomach. I couldn't even blush the way I normally did. Instead, I just turned cold. Maybe everybody noticed, because after that, no one bothered me about my dad again.

By spring, life had settled into a predictable pattern. I had friends, could skip rope, and I was doing well in school. Even though I wasn't fully Swedish I sure looked it, which must have helped in some way. I had a blonde bob cut with bangs and two new milk-fed front teeth poking through my gums. I know this from pictures Mom took of me on our balcony (six floors up, it slanted slightly downwards). In the pictures, I am always smiling. But, in spite of my wholesome appearance, the cracks must have been detectable. This is the only way I could explain what happened one day at the end of the semester. At the time I told myself it was just a coincidence, a question of being at the wrong place at the wrong time, and yet somewhere in the back of my mind, I feared that I had been branded by my dad's disappearance.

I was the last one out of school that day. The doors were made of solid wood and they were so heavy the only way to exit was to drop the door and rush out before it slammed shut on your limbs. I walked into the empty school yard, across the ball squares, towards Anna-Lena, our daycare lady, where my little brother was waiting. The distance wasn't that great, but it felt far somehow, because as soon as I passed the hedges, different rules applied. For example, at school I was allowed to chew my pencils, or at any rate, the teacher didn't say anything about how I destroyed my school-issued HP pens. If you bit anything wooden at Anna-Lena's house, like a Popsicle stick, she went apeshit. Her ability to detect biters was uncanny. If she handed you a Piggelin ice-cream, even if she never saw you eat any of it, she'd be there the moment you licked the last drop off to yank the stick out of your mouth, before you got a chance to graze your teeth on the wood. She would always give you her reason as well.

"Don't chew the sticks! I hate it, my skin crawls, it gives me the heebie jeebies!"

I didn't get very far that day before I saw three boys from my class bundled off to the side by the hawthorn trees. The velvety leaves had just opened and they cast enough of a shadow that I couldn't quite see who the boys were, not until they started walking towards me. They were carrying sticks, but boys with sticks wasn't unusual and I was not afraid, not right away, because I knew all of them.

"Hej!" I waved. None of them replied. Instead they shouted—I can't remember what—and jabbed their sticks into the air. They moved towards me, spreading out, and I instinctively turned around and ran back towards school. The main entrance was too far off so I headed towards the basement entrance of the janitor's office. There was a set of stairs on one side and a ramp on the other for deliveries. This seemed like a good place to hide even though I regretted it as soon as I got to the bottom step and realized I was trapped. I resisted pounding on the door because I didn't want to bother the staff, but as soon as the rocks started flying, I did anyway. When the lights didn't come on, I jumped across to the other side where I wasn't immediately visible. The boys came running up and hung themselves over the railing, stabbing their sticks towards my head. One of them pulled back his arm and aimed his stick at me like a spear, but when it came down, it only bounced weakly off my thigh. Anticipating what I was sure would come next—punches and kicks— I balled up and covered my face with my hands. There was a drain in the corner and a scabby growth of moss spreading up the wall. The boys moved around the railing and I pressed my nose into the dampness of the moss and closed my eyes. But then, things went quiet. I looked up between my fingers. They were standing at the top of the steps looking huge and shadowy, but they had tossed everything available to them and were empty-handed. Seeing them frozen, I said something. I can't remember what. Maybe I pleaded or maybe I had enough adrenaline going to tell them off. It wouldn't have been the first time my temper made me bold. Whatever it was, something changed. Two of them walked away and the last one stood there, hesitating. I wasn't sure if he wanted the game to keep going or if he felt concerned, but he gave me a long look before he walked away.

I sat there until I couldn't hear anything except the magpies. I peeked over the edge. My hands trembled but I wasn't angry. Only scared. I remembered what Dad had told me when I started daycare and encountered my first bully: "If someone hits you, hit back." Mom had told me that hitting back was never a good idea but secretly I had agreed with Dad. Hitting back was better. I vowed then and there that I would never let anyone beat on me. But nobody hit me that day, nobody had even touched me. Perhaps defending myself was harder than he had made it seem. By the time I walked over the yard, crossed the hedge, and walked over to Anna-Lena's, I had already started erasing the boys' faces out of my mind, which is how I was able to go back the next day and pretend as if nothing had happened. And in the end maybe nothing did happen, only the threat of something. And how do you protect yourself against that?

AND THREE MORE

Rose Camara

Phoebe settled into her therapist's couch and closed her eyes, bracing for the journey through the dank recesses of her mind. She was determined to unearth what she'd lost.

She took three deep, calming breaths and visualized donning her caving helmet with built-in searchlight: a shield against what she might encounter and a star illuminating her path.

The cave—jagged, dark, and dripping—filled in around her. At the sight of the wooden barricade, askew as if assembled in haste, her crowbar appeared in her hand. The only way back was through, she had learned. No shortcuts. Every time it was the same.

She pried apart weathered planks, rusted nails giving way. This portal between past and present was easier to open now. Removing a single board no longer made her brain sing with fatigue.

Through the opening, life's detritus still decorated the cave like lilies on a pond: free weights, past loves, the pool where she had lifeguarded in her twenties.

She maneuvered her way through the barrier between present and past. The helmet protected her from scrapes and blows, but its continuous squeeze was hard to bear.

Beyond the portal, she rested, hands on knees, eyes closed, breathing hard. When she straightened, her eyes swept the surroundings as they always did. Their last family picture hung on one craggy wall. Phoebe, 4, in a gingham dress. Jackson, 6, in a raglan tee, weeks before he died. She saw the portrait in her mother's apartment every Sunday, but never in the cave—until now.

Three deep, calming breaths.

She scaled slabs of slimy rock, using both hands to hoist herself from one to the next, past campus parties, study nights, and the bathroom stall where she'd hidden from roommates to release torrents of tears. A phase she'd fully explored. She hiked on.

She passed her old gym, where she'd worked out day after day to chase more reps, more weight, more hours. Grimacing through every injury, every heartache. Pushing to be faster, stronger. Until she blew her knee out and had to quit competitive swimming for good. She had never been weaker, more panicked.

Three deep, calming breaths.

The rubble became hard-packed snow and the air sharpened, as her childhood toboggan hill appeared. She conjured an ice axe and toe picks to prevent her sliding back. To her right, her father beat a vicious dog off a small child. A ferocity in his voice that shook her still.

He had saved the kid's life when Phoebe was 8. She pressed on.

Past the snow, Phoebe hesitated, knowing what was next. She hated wet clothes, even metaphorically. But there was no other way through the pool of water in front of her.

Three deep, calming breaths. And three more.

She wriggled her feet, planted firmly on the ground. Despite this pool she was safe and dry, just trying to see the other side, see herself.

She plunged one foot into the water, and the other. The water lapped at her ankles, then her knees, thighs, and hips. She shivered but didn't stop. When her legs emerged again, her jeans were pasted on. She felt the water fall away from her body and relished the knowledge she could do hard things.

A welcome mat appeared at her feet, brown and worn. Past it, the front door of the family home. The door opened, and the cave's damp funk was muted by brewing coffee and baked goods. A framed picture of Jackson stood next to an arrangement of white roses and daisies on the kitchen table. People milled about in black, carrying tissues and finger sandwiches.

She stopped for him, to feel him: the brother she knew in her bones—as his deputy in free-range adventures—and who she didn't know at all—because his spirit had been snuffed before he'd grown into his skin. A surge of love rocked her, and she rode it until it passed.

Three deep, calming breaths.

The house fell away.

The cave tightened and darkened around Phoebe as it always did with unexplored terrain. The roof dripped incessantly. Droplets magnified the cobwebs she swiped away with her fingers. She was grateful for her light. It never gave out, even when she wanted to. The floor was littered with soggy stuffies, army figurines, and paper snowflakes. A wall calendar was turned to June, featuring a picture of a peaceful lake, edged with willows. Branches dipped into the water like toes safely tethered to their trunk.

June 6th was circled in thick, black ink. The calendar was unfamiliar, but the date was unforgettable.

The darkness opened to a grassy hill. The roar of the river just over the rise made her chest heave. She covered her ears and stood, motionless. She should have seen it coming.

Three deep, calming—

She clenched her fists and strode over the hill.

On the other side, a dark-haired child sat at the river's edge amidst driftwood and river rock. She wore grey sweatpants paired with a gingham dress and black gumboots. A kid ready for anything.

Almost anything.

The child's arms were wrapped around her knees, her face hidden within. Her clothes were soaked below the waist, dripping.

"No, no, no." Phoebe whispered. She held her breath, abandoning her mantra entirely, and backed away: one step, two, three. But the child looked up.

Both their ragged breaths quickened, an interminable call and response, until Phoebe sat beside her 4-year-old self.

The child said, "I wasn't fast enough... strong enough. Couldn't stop him... couldn't hold... I couldn't..."

The rushing river amplified in Phoebe's ears. Bile rose in her throat. She saw Jackson's small fingers slipping through her even smaller ones.

She had been there?

She had been there.

Her chest tightened.

Leave, she thought. *Go!*

But adult Phoebe looked into the child's eyes instead. They were weighed down by shame. Phoebe lifted her young self into her lap, stroked her knotted hair.

The child's hitching breath drew Phoebe's attention to her own.

She took three deep, calming breaths. And three more. And three more.

HATCHLING

Tara Ross

Today the first hatchling emerges from the gravel and dying maple leaves. A rough, moody pebble to match the overcast sky and heaviness of the coming season.

Mason, always keen to avoid his highchair, spots it while retrieving a catnip-stuffed baby sock for Fuzzy. Truth be told, the cat should get the credit for this discovery, but rarely is credit given where it's deserved. "Mama, they're here!" Mason says, pushing a chubby finger into the hole of our screen door.

I offer a "That's nice" while passing the relish to Gary. My half-hearted response only seems to spur Mason's enthusiasm. He yanks on the door, and Fuzzy hunches forward, ready to pounce.

"Not yet, please. We're still eating," I say, curling my finger for his return, but now Cedric is under the table, army-crawling toward his brother. My eldest, Nora, stands, her gaze pacing between me, her dad, and the back door as if a travelling cosmetic-mobile has appeared and not an abandoned baby turtle.

"It'll still be there when we finish." Finish dinner, finish cleaning, and finish the talk.

Gary and I have been avoiding this conversation for weeks, although we both agreed after my perilous drive home from work that tonight, before school starts back up, would be best. I look to him for support, but he stuffs half his hot dog into his mouth and shrugs.

Cedric rises from his crawl and plants his face onto the screen. "What if it gets lost?"

"It's a turtle. It will still be there after—"

"It could go the wrong way." Nora presses into the table much the same way I do when frustrated. "What if it goes on the road?"

Gary holds up a finger while he swallows, then says, "Nobody needs to freak out." He chugs back his milk and wipes his mouth with the back of his hand. He then rises, placing his glass an inch shy of his placemat, and walks to the front hall. The children follow him like baby ducks, while I watch a drip slide down the side of his glass. It will seep into the wood. It will leave another ring.

"It's still supper time," I say to the empty chairs, shuffled to varying distances from the table. Cedric's milk is untouched. Mason's reward chips wait on his napkin, and my hot dog—the last one left on the serving tray—seems to ask why we are the only ones left.

I pour Mason's chips onto my plate and fold his oil-stained napkin in half and then into quarters. When Gary returns, flip-flops on his feet, children in tow, his glass is in my hand, milk drip gone.

Gary nudges Fuzzy back as the children escape into the backyard and then he sighs toward the table—maybe at the untouched hot dog, or the empty ketchup bottle, or maybe even at the strain in my jaw as I pick at the crumbs no one else seems to notice. "We can talk to them after dinner's cleaned up," he says.

"Sure."

"Take a minute. I've got the kids."

"Sure." *Wouldn't want to lose a turtle*, I almost add.

The screen slaps shut, but the laughter and indifference stream through—Mason counting off each hatchling that claws into the light, Gary directing as the never-failing foreman of fun. No one is judging the momma turtle for leaving her babies behind. Nobody complains about whether they had enough snacks way down in their hole. The mental fortitude of their turtle matriarch—who must also know her failings—is not even a passing thought.

Maybe saving these tiny lives will dampen what is to come.

The soundtrack of their rescue mission guides me to the kitchen. I fill the kettle and fight hard to leave the tower of dirty Tupperware in place. I play Tetris with chipped Ikea glasses and Mother's Day mugs until I find the gold-flaked tea cup and saucer I reserve for the heaviest of days—the cup my mother swore got her through fifty years of marriage and seventy-six years of life.

This is not a cup I choose lightly, however it's the reminder Gary needs to not skirt this situation again. He does not want me using it as my mother did, deepening the ring left by her whiskey. I fill it mostly with boiled water and a chamomile-mint blend, but leave room for enough honey to disguise the bitterness of my new medication.

Back at the supper table, I raise the cup to my lips and allow the cleansing steam to mask the smell of boiled meat and soured condiments. The fading light of early evening closes in on the table, scolding me for years of grime and unsaved drips, highlighting fork scrapes and crayon tantrums, rebuking me for not scrubbing hard enough. I pray to have just one ounce of the mental fortitude of that snapper in the creek.

The screen squeaks open, and I stiffen, waiting for another sigh from Gary, but it's Nora. My perceptive Nora. "Mom?" She kicks off her shoes and settles into the seat next to me. "We don't know what to do."

I place my teacup on its saucer and try to brighten my eyes. "What do you mean, sweets?"

"Crows are circling." She looks at the tiny pill next to my tea, instead of out the back door.

I want to tell her they've been circling for weeks, waiting for this day. That only a handful of the prehistoric blobs will survive this exodus. However, I also want to be a good mother. At least for this moment. "They'll be fine. Your dad's out there. He'll come up with something."

"But their mom isn't here, and they look so scared."

"Do they?" I wonder how she could know. Is it the darkness of their pin-tip eyes or the way they scuffle about through an invisible maze? Could they feel as lost as I do, lacking in instincts I should have in spades? And what of their mother? Does she sense what is to come? How both our children will wail when the birds swoop down?

"Mom?" Although Nora's hand is light on my arm, it does the job of drawing me back. My always perceptive Nora. I remember to smile. I look to the clouds, willing this endless weight to release for a moment. *What should I do? What can I say?* This is not the time for childish rhymes about sticks and stones, or for platitudes about the fragility of life. She understands pain takes different shapes and that few of us escape life without exit wounds. But before tonight, she was one of the lucky ones. Unscathed by life.

I take a strand of her caramel hair and slide it through my fingers before placing it behind her ear. "You'll need to trust the journey."

Her lips press together and then quiver for a sliver of time. I expect questions or a new argument about the turtles. Instead, she reaches for my hair, slides her fingers through it, and tucks it behind my ear.

She watches me eat stale potato chips and sip at my tea. She comforts Fuzzy as he stalks between us and the screen. Although she tries to clear the dishes, I hold her hand at the table with me. I can tell by the redness in her eyelids that she knows what is to come. She is so strong. I'll need to remember this when I wake each morning.

The shadow of something winged swoops low across our backyard and silences the boys. They all look to me. Momma. Wife. Gifted—or perhaps afflicted—by an instinct to protect all the things I love.

Nora inches sideways on her seat, feet pivoted to join them, but she looks to me, waiting.

"You want to do something?" I say more as a statement than a question.

She nods, yet hesitates in her seat. Her red eyes dart between me and the shadows in the sky. "How long will you be gone?" She says just above a whisper, now holding my gaze, face strong, shoulders back.

"No," I say, reaching across the table for my hot dog. "I'm not letting you..." I go to take a bite, but my stomach won't allow it. Instead, I rip my dinner in half and then into quarters and eighths, spongy meat collecting under my nails as I decide what she will not take on, but the words won't come. I shake my head to hold back the much too familiar sting, but her stoicism—it breaks me, the maturity of her acceptance. This is not okay. I will not be the first scar in her life. I toss the meat chunks into the leftover chips and push back from the table, my eyes carefully evading hers.

"I get it, Mom." She stands, already almost my height, hands pressed again into the table. "I'm getting ready for the journey," she says with an authority she shouldn't possess.

"That was for the turtles." *Not for the things I can't figure out how to love properly.* "This." I glare down at my pill. "This is different."

"Maybe not," she says, and I recognize so much of myself in her pressed lips.

I skirt my attention back to the table, and strive to take in a full breath. It's not so bad, the aftermath of a meal—stacking and rinsing plates, replacing caps on bottles, gathering up the crumbs. Still, even this small task feels impossible today. I can't stay like this. Eventually, I'll end up back in my car, ignoring the curves, seeking my final creek again.

Instead of heeding to the demands of the table, I pinch the oval pill, rolling it between my pointer and thumb. My tea has cooled and what remains will be sweet. I swallow it down and finally say, "Less than a month." The time it will take for the honey and bitterness to get along. I hope.

She holds out her hands for my plate. For what I intended to be the crows' feast.

I tilt my head towards the screen door. "Takes all of us, right?"

She nods, shuffles back into her shoes, and pulls the door open for us. I want so desperately to match her small but true smile, but that will take time. Gary waves for the boys to stop their aerial assault. I look up to the clouds and the still circling birds, then experience a different weight as two small bodies latch onto my legs.

Gary mouths *are you okay?* I show him my dinner plate and a face I no longer want to be stoic. A third, then a fourth weight embraces me, and it no longer feels impossible to breathe.

We spend the next ten minutes shepherding hatchlings to safety. Then we return home to embark on the impossible conversation of how not everyone will make it through life unscathed, even if we're the ones throwing those sticks and stones.

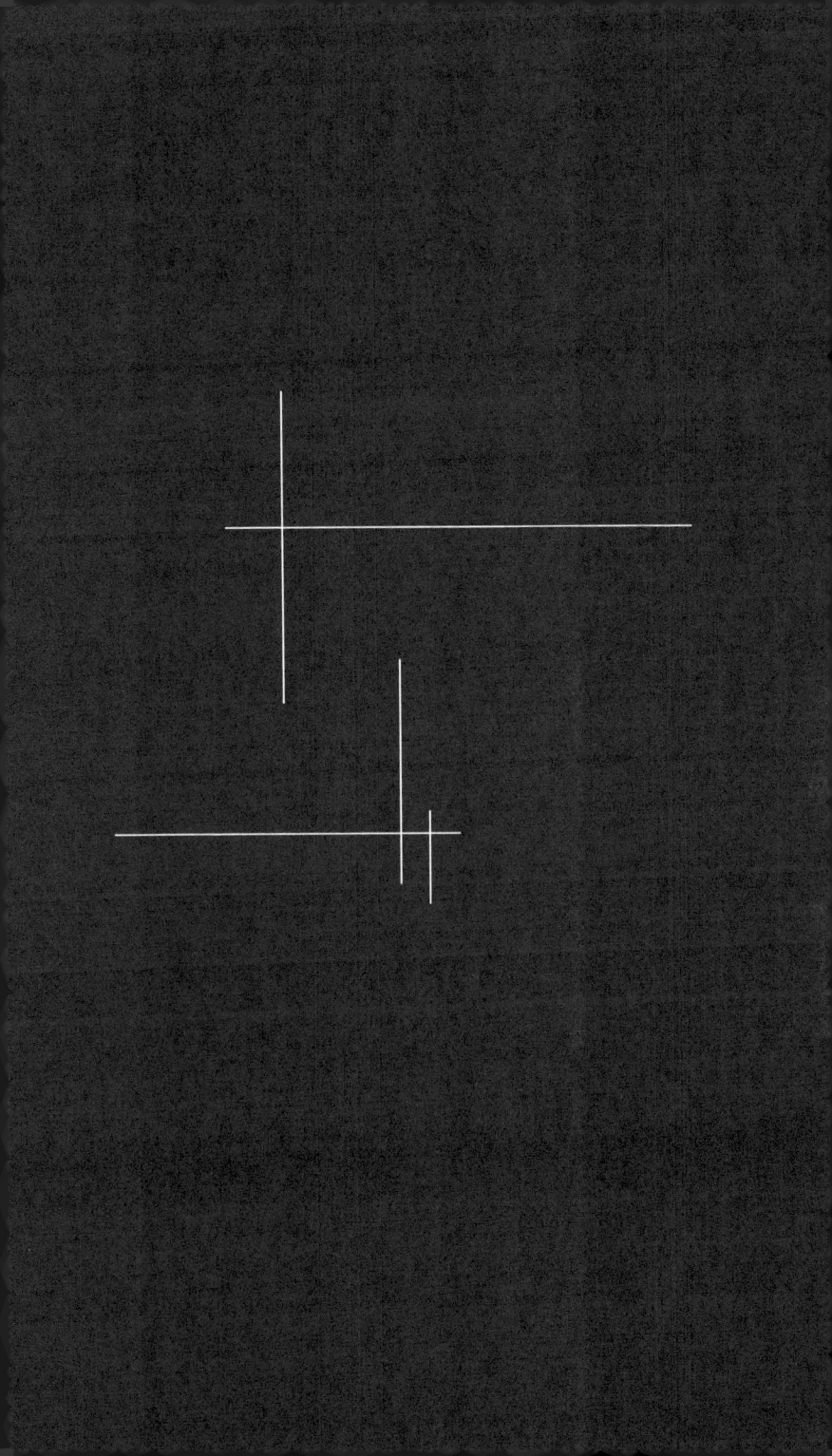

THE SCAVENGER'S GARDEN

Nikki Berreth

A surge of panic washed over me as I followed Ronni over the threshold and gave my arms one more vigorous scrub with my palms. Mother was a hawk and could spot the telltale signs of chain link gawking from a mile away and I was already maxed out on the chore chart—what consequence could she bestow me with this time?

I mimicked Ronni's composure as Mom asked, "Did you trade for bread?"

Ronnie plopped two loaves onto the counter and Mom eyed her. "Only cost two credits today."

"Thirty-eight credits remaining," I added, not wanting her to mistake my silence for guilt.

Mom's eyebrows quickly disappeared under her wispy bangs. "Larson must be in a good mood. I heard his daughter is partnering with the Wickers boy—that will make a nice union." She barely looked at either of us as she turned back to her food preparation. "Wash up. Breakfast will be ready soon."

Relief accompanied a rush of breath from my lungs, and Ronni shot me an annoyed look. Did she hear that?

"Oh girls," Mom quipped as we started down the hallway, "gawking at the gardens will get us all in trouble. Do better."

Ronni's eyes rolled in my direction and she held a finger to her lips to keep me from laughing, but I didn't feel jolly. The heat was rising in my face and I silently reprimanded myself for giving into desire, but my guilt quickly turned into frustration. We entered the bathroom, and I mumbled, "Why can't we all have gardens?"

Ronni sighed and swiftly pushed the door closed. "Because we are stone masons," she hissed as she squirted a bit of soap in my hands, "not farmers." She began massaging her hands together.

"They aren't farmers either!" I angrily rubbed at my hand, feeling the soap slip and slide between my palms as I thought of all the well-washed women jovially tending the gardens in their giant obnoxious hats—it's never sunny enough for a hat that size. "I could be twice the gardener they are and I'd share," I spat at the mirror.

Ronni huffed at me, and we washed in silence, taking turns at the basin. My sister moved around me like I was a hot steam that could burn her. I grabbed the hand towel from my stone basket—well, it was less a basket and more a pot with a drainage hole in the bottom. Two months ago, I began my fifteenth trip around the sun, and with it came the expectation to contribute to the stone mason economy. You slowly work through different styles of stone masonry until you uncover your strengths. I'll tell you one thing... my strength does not lie in the stone pot.

We dragged ourselves back to the kitchen, where my parents were already nestled at the table. My mom gestured wildly with a pot of berry jam while regaling my dad with a story of the custom pineapple ornament she had chiselled for a client—she was the best chisel-worker in Rocklum—that resulted in even more custom requests.

Ronnie and I joined the table without a word and helped ourselves. My dad must have traded at work today, because sitting in an ornate stone bowl was a neat pile of tiny tomatoes. Their deep red skins looked about to burst. I reached for one and popped it between my lips. The first bite was a surprise—juice gushing into every crevice of my mouth. My eyes closed involuntarily and my mind became quiet until I heard, "Guess where the girls were today."

My eyes sprang open and I could see that my father already knew the answer, disapproval deep in the lines of his face. I gulped, but his gaze bore deep into Ronni. She was two years my senior and should know better than to let her little sister gawk at the gardens.

I tried to think of something to say, but he had already launched into his mini sermon. "Listen girls. You know that we all..." My mind wandered as my tongue worked a tomato seed from my teeth. Then, an idea struck me. Carefully, I grabbed my small cloth napkin and, under the cover of wiping my mouth, I dropped the seed onto the woven fabric. My dad was now lecturing my sister about her duty as the older sibling, my mother nodding along with a grave expression on her face. I eyed the tomatoes again and quickly stuffed the food on my plate into my mouth. I palmed a few more tomatoes, shoving another in my mouth and two into the cloth napkin. With deft fingers, I folded the napkin into my pocket.

"Done! Can I go outside now?" My dad stopped talking, a blank look on his face as he tried to remember where he was in his speech and simultaneously processed what I just asked him. My mother nodded that I could go.

I hustled through the quiet streets of Rocklum. Breakfast was a typical resting point each day as everyone gathered with their families. With the empty street and my favourite short-cuts, I was out of the community and halfway to Woodlum before you could ask, "Where did Libby say she was going?"

The dense canopy of trees enveloped me in a darkness that my eyes still needed to adjust to. I slowed and strained my ears to listen for Woodlum inhabitants, and in the distance I heard the high pitch of children's voices. I bet Max was with them. As I emerged into a small clearing of low shrubs dotted with red berries and jiggling under the lazy fingers of the Woodlum kids, I quickly located Max.

"Lib!" Max's mouth stretched wide to reveal purple teeth. "You gotta try these berries. They are delicious." I reached out to the berries and stroked one with my finger. A wave of jealousy came over me. "It's only their first year, so we don't need to report them yet." She was referring to the government's expectation to inventory all raw goods—found or created.

"Maybe you don't need to report it at all. Save all the berries for yourself and you won't even need the market anymore."

"Hush!" Max swatted at me. "That's consequential talk." Her eyes scanned over the others to see if they were listening. "Besides, dummy, to meet our calorie needs, we would need to eat literal buckets of berries. Forestry is tough work and we need to buy meats, bread, and potatoes." She offered me another perfect berry.

I popped both in my mouth and swayed at the burst of flavour. "What we need is to build our own garden." Max grunted her skepticism. "No, really. Nothing in the law says that we can't build our own garden."

"But you can't buy seeds, bulbs, or anything to plant, so what would be the point?"

"We don't always need to BUY those things." I dragged the napkin from my pocket and unveiled the tomatoes to her.

"So?"

I gawked at her insolence. "So, these tomatoes have," I looked around me to see if anyone was listening before I hissed, "seeeeeeds." There must have been a twinkle in my eye because her face suddenly turned serious. "Follow me, please." I waved for her to walk with me.

Maxine took one look at the berry patch and the children

before she trailed after me. I led her through the trees, bending low under large cedar roots, and climbing over decaying nursery stumps. I checked behind me to see if she was keeping pace, but she was so close I could wrap an arm around her. Sometimes I forgot this was her home.

We emerged into a small meadow with a lazy brook and a weeping willow standing guard on its edge. I ducked beneath a long curtain of weeping leaves and crawled under its protection, stopping briefly to rest a hand on its bark. Max followed suit and whispered an honour. It was a Woodlum custom to connect with the trees whenever practical.

I continued to the other side of the canopy and ducked once more under the curtain to stand before a giant glacial erratic. The stone stood nine feet in height and resembled a wood block, like a child's toy. I ran two quick steps before scurrying up the rock face and hoisting myself onto the top and into the weak sunlight. I closed my eyes and felt the gentle warmth reflecting off the granite top. A grunt made me look over the side to witness Max, red-faced and struggling to get up. I smirked. This stone—my forte—was out of place in the middle of the forest.

I reached down and grabbed her shirt collar, hoisting her over the edge. "Et voilà!" I hollered as my hand swept to the large flat top of the rock.

Her eyes widened. The top was nearly twelve feet by fourteen feet of flat surface and covered in misshapen stone pots filled with dirt from the forest floor and small green shoots. "How?" was the only word she could manage.

"Well, as you know, I'm learning stone masonry and

its…" I gestured to one of the ugliest pots. "It's not going well."

Maxine's head bobbed rhythmically as she looked at all the pots. "And the plants? This could get you into trouble."

"Nope. I didn't break any rules. These plants came from seeds," I took the tomatoes out of my pocket again, "and shoots." I couldn't stop the smile from spreading on my face. "This," I gestured to one of the green shoots, "is garlic from a sprouting clove that my mom tossed into the bin. And this," I fingered the ragged edge of another pot, "this is an asparagus shoot I found while on a walk through Woodlum."

"How do you know it's asparagus? It looks like a fern."

"I found a book." I lifted my head triumphantly, daring her to defy my resourcefulness.

She looked away and took in the pots. "I'm scared to ask what else is in these."

"All gained similarly. And now," I gestured again to the napkin, "I have tomatoes!"

She gave me a skeptical look, and I knew she was about to get down to business. "So what? You are just going to keep making pots and growing things here?"

My head dropped to my chest. "Ugh. No. My dad is giving up on me and the pots so I can't make any more, but…" I eyed her hopefully, "the roots of these plants will stop growing once they find they can't move further down. They need more room to grow."

"Meaning there is no point to this." She threw her hands up in frustration.

"That's where you are wrong," I rounded on her. "We

have the means to build a proper garden bed up here, but I will need your help."

"Oh, boy," hands on her hips, "tell me what we need."

It took three days to pilfer all the supplies. Max needed to extricate enough rough-cut wood destined for the junk pile, and I needed to lug enough stones from Rocklum to create our masterpiece.

My mother commented twice on how the pockets of my pants seemed to stretch. "What are you getting up to?"

I smiled. "I promise it doesn't involve any gawking." She shook her head. Truth be told, I stopped briefly to examine the height of the garden beds so we could build ours similarly. It was extra brief because I didn't see the gardener in her giant hat eyeing me suspiciously.

Max's parents questioned her repeated and unexplained disappearances over these days, but she shook them off with excuses for surveying unknown parts of the woods for more berry bushes. It seemed believable, so they didn't press further.

Once we had all the materials, it took another day to construct the bed of sticks and stones, weave the branches of the weeping willow through them, and haul enough soil up the rock face to fill it. After careful placement of our shoots, seeds, and sprouts, we made a quick schematic of what was where. I studied my plant book to record how often we needed to water each plant.

We were beat, but as we gazed at our new garden, a wave of exhilaration hit us. We had almost everything we needed...

Except for time.

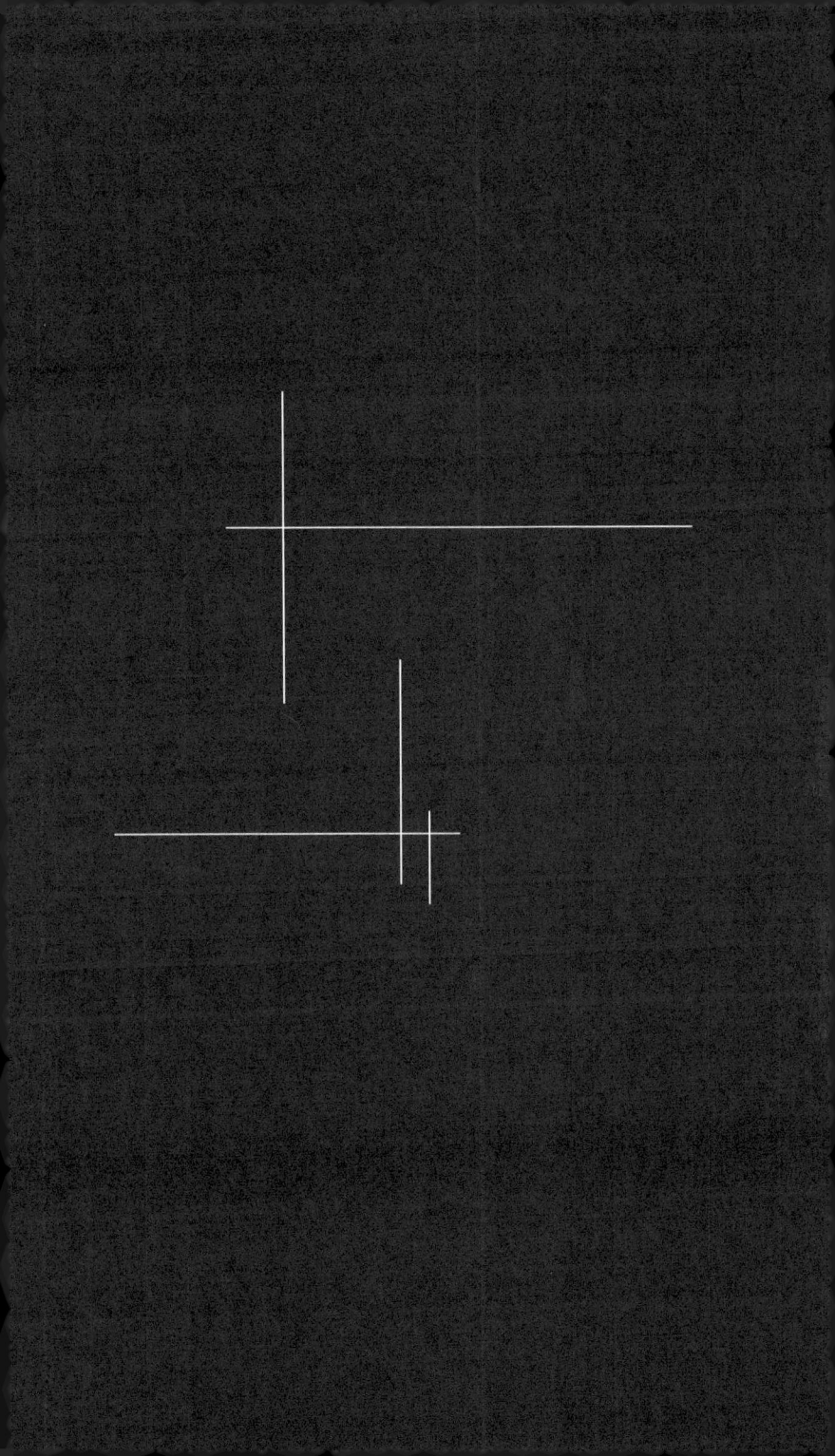

KEEPSAKES

Katrine Raymond

Heart trouble ran through the Delaneys like a curse. Jim sat on his mom's blue striped couch, pulled a shoebox from underneath, and wiped sweat from his nose. His heartbeat raced as he lifted the box. Jim had inherited his father's bad heart. He pulled off the shoebox lid: hundreds of bottle caps. Mom didn't keep regular old lady stuff around. No Royal Doulton figurines or boxes of love letters tied with string. Instead, it was mostly junk. Rusty old bottle openers and coasters snatched from bars closed down decades ago. Sticks and stones. Twos of things. She wasn't a pack-rat, just old and tired, and unsure what to do with life.

Jim ran his hand through the bottle caps, enjoying the tinny sound.

"*Stop it*," Evie said. "You're such a kid, Jimmy." She was ten years older than Jim, and when she was a teenager, quick and cruel, she used to call him *the mistake*. Jim stood up and steadied himself. He took a few seconds to catch his breath. The air in the house was stale. For a while now, he'd been feeling these small but noticeable thumps in his heart as it wavered from its usual beat. Some days it felt like his heart was a small mammal, writhing in his chest.

When Evie had called a month ago, Jim wasn't surprised at the news. Mom had been saying that she should have died years ago. And she *should* have—but she'd outlived Dad and her priest. It was Evie's other piece of news that moved him out of his torpor: "We're meeting next month to go through Mom's stuff. You're coming." Evie was the eldest, with her ordering people around and I-told-you-sos. Jim did whatever she said.

But not this time, he wouldn't *stop it*. He sat down and started rattling the bottle caps harder. The clacking calmed him, caps smooth and cool on his fingertips.

There was so much detritus in the house that the job would take days. Neither of them had been at the house for a while. Mom had been in and out of the hospital for months, and before that she'd invited herself over to their places for Christmas and Easter. They hadn't known what to expect. At first, it seemed easy. Evie brought a box of green garbage bags and a plan to fill them quickly. But then, as they began turning over chairs and rifling through the fridge, they began to notice the notes.

Pinned on a hat: *I wore this on Easter in 1944, the year I met your father. The peonies are showy and I knew it at the time. Only a young girl with dark hair and long eyelashes could pull this off. How ridiculous!*

Taped under an ottoman: *Cousin Earl, the famous American weatherman, put his feet on this while visiting. Hadn't seen him in person since he was five. It was pouring rain that day. He was wearing striped socks. What unusually big feet.*

Even in the freezer, a strange chunk of cloudy ice: *From the ice storm of 1986. Power out for three days and temperatures down near 0 degrees Fahrenheit. I had to burn books — sacrilege!*

Evie dumped the ice in the toilet to melt.

"I know these notes," Jim said.

Evie cocked an eyebrow.

The last time Jim visited Mom in the hospital, she'd been diagnosed with diverticulitis. She'd told him that her list was getting longer. At first he didn't know what she meant.

Diverticulitis. It sounded like an ill-gotten venereal disease.

Everything else was wrong with her too. Over the years, her body had succumbed to all sorts of assaults, her sadness and fear turning to blood clots and food allergies.

She'd developed lupus and celiac disease and diabetes and a long list of small, as-of-yet undiagnosed, ailments. Not that those were any less real.

It felt like her gut was exploding, she said, as her hands smoothed the thin hospital sheet.

"It's just the swelling," Jim reassured her. Nothing to worry about, in itself. "This old horse will live forever," she said.

A part of him figured because she said it, it must be true.

"Can you write me a note?" she asked him.

"Sure." At first he thought she wanted him to send her mail at the hospital.

But she handed him a pen and a small note pad. She meant right now. "I need another note." Her eyesight was almost gone.

She begin to dictate:

From the dance at the church hall. That night I danced with your father to make Jimmy Reed jealous. At the end of the night that handsome young man who became your father said I should phone him—

Jim was mystified, pinning it on old age. She asked him to stop there. "The nurse will finish for me," she said. "She knows what comes next."

Mom was the youngest of thirteen children, so getting her way was her birthright. Lucky thirteen, dad joked when he asked her to marry him on the thirteenth of March, so many years ago. It had been a Friday, which he said was extra lucky—the stuff of family lore.

On that last visit to the hospital, Jim felt smothered. Mom wasn't big on guilt trips but he managed to feel guilty anyway. She was never bitter about her pain and relentless fatigue. She was unusually honest for a mother. She told them when something hurt. But just her sickness was enough to make him feel bad. When he left the hospital that day, he pulled out of the parking lot and peered out the rear window for one last look. Mom in the window, both arms waving wildly, used Kleenex flying out her housecoat sleeves like doves from a magician's waistcoat.

After Dad's first heart attack, they figured Mom's health would decline too, but she surprised them. Her digestion improved as his appetite waned. She began to do the grocery shopping again. He seemed to understand her better, acknowledging her aches and pains as something more than imaginary. But when he died from a second attack three weeks later, her indigestion came back, and her colour turned yellow.

Now Jim put down the shoebox. Evie grabbed it and began to dump the bottle caps into her growing bag of unsalvageable garbage. "Wait," Jim said. "I want to read the note."

It was peeking from the bottom of the box.

These bottle caps number all of the soda pops and beer I drank without your father. Most were from the years after he died. But one was on the night you were conceived, Jimmy — Red Deer.

December 2, 1963. It was cold that night. Her husband away. It didn't take Annette much effort to convince Jimmy Reed to go out with her. On her part, it had required a babysitter and a series of small lies. After years of distance, all it took was one quick phone call and a few memories.

"Bundle up," Jimmy said. "Aren't you the girl who grew up in the Great White North?"

Annette smiled with half of her mouth. "It was Kirkland Lake, not the Yukon."

"That hair of yours is still spun gold." He wound her best cabled scarf around and around her until it covered her mouth and nose. "And I hear the price of gold is going up." He tucked the end in gently and tapped her nose.

She grinned underneath because she knew he wouldn't see it. Her husband would never say anything ridiculous like that. She didn't even know what he meant. Her hair was auburn, at best. But all she could think of was Rapunzel and Jimmy Reed's wide shoulders.

"I know a warm spot," he said.

He drove her to a sheltered grove under the bridge. His truck was full of shells and stones, sticks and books and dull pencils, nothing like her husband's neat Chevy. He was right. The spot was warm, protected by the bridge on one side and a row of cedars on the other, their soft branches blocking the wind.

He handed her a bottle of beer. She wasn't used to drinking alcohol.

"Just one," he said. "To warm you up."

She was here for one thing. She didn't want that one thing turning into more.

She ran her glove over the deer dancing on the label. She took two sips and nestled the bottle into the snow.

Afterwards, Jimmy lit a cigarette and told her that he was moving to Toronto as he played with her flaxen hair. But Annette already knew this and was glad. Her husband came back two days later from the ice fishing trip.

She ended up naming the baby Jimmy, as a thank you.

Jim opened Mom's desk drawer. It was empty, except for a few paper clips and dust balls along the edge. He ran his hand along the smooth pine bottom until his finger ran up against cardboard. A faded black and white business card was sitting in the back. Jim read, "Steve's Plumbing: We love going down the drain." There was a note.

From the dance at the church hall. That night I danced with your father to make Jimmy Reed jealous. At the end of the night that handsome young man who became your father said I should phone him. He handed me this business card and grinned. I called the plumber. It took me weeks to figure out that your father's phone number was actually scrawled on the back of the card in pencil.

TS7-4322 was scrawled on the back of the card in Dad's chicken scratch hand.

Jim picked up the phone receiver. Mom had loved her old rotary, unable to part with it until the end. There was still a dial tone. Should he call the number? Is that what she meant for him to do? But in the middle of the dial, a note poked out of the plastic dial cover. He pulled it out.

I named you Jimmy, after my first love. The note was written on the back of an old beer label, faded but still legible. Mom had never been to Alberta. Red Deer was the name of a beer. A slim red deer stood with one of its forelegs bent, as if he were dancing. He kept reading.

I wanted another little one, to be with Evie when we were gone. I wanted you. And by that point, we'd tried for years. We always thought it was me, being sick and all—but inside, I knew it wasn't.

"Did Mom keep any old photo albums?" Jim asked. He felt his heart beat skittery again.

"No," Evie said, "She didn't take photos." Mom had been partially blind by the end. Evie walked away, but suddenly turned around. "Well, there's one." She fished around in the garbage bag she was holding and handed him one faded Polaroid print. "I found it in Mom's nightstand." But there weren't any smiling faces. Just a cup of milky tea with tiny bubbles on the surface in the shape of a heart.

A small note on the back read, *These bubbles appeared after you were born.* Jim wasn't sure, but he figured she meant him.

Jim paced back and forth across the hallway. "Slow down," Evie said. "You're just like Dad, always rushing around. No wonder you've got his heart."

"These notes," Jim said carefully. "Can you keep them when you find them?"

Evie glared at him. "There's a note on practically every damn thing in this house."

"You can throw the stuff away," he said. "But the notes..."

"It's ridiculous," Evie said. "She did it on purpose." She pulled out a hard candy and starting sucking on it. "She wanted to make it impossible for us to get rid of anything." She had every right to be angry. Hadn't Annette been a lousy mother? Always sick and making Evie play mother when Jim was small.

Inside an old prescription bottle: *Your father was a good man. The worst thing about him was that he didn't really believe I was sick. He said it couldn't be that bad. I guess he didn't want to believe it. Maybe that's what killed him in the end. He finally got sick himself and his heart just broke.*

Dad was big on tall tales. His thirty-pound lake trout. His assist that won the Grandview tournament. He'd pretended that Mom had never been sick a day in her life. He'd pretended that he, too, was a perfect specimen. He'd pretended that the ten-year gap between kids was a god-given waiting period until they were "ready." He'd pretended that Jim was his son.

Inside an empty glass bottle: *I never saw Jimmy Reed again, but he used to mail me herbal teas and odd liniments you could only find in special shops in Toronto. He sent little notes with each package over the years. "Lotions and potions," he wrote. "To help you feel better, or at least give you a smile." Somehow he understood my sickness better than anyone.*

Like his father, Jim used to think his mother's illnesses were embellished, if not completely fabricated. But in those last years the doctors confirmed it: the stomach troubles, the lupus. They said she'd been through a lot.

Next, Jim found the obituary in the bathroom. Jimmy Reed died of old age. In his sleep.

Jim sat back down, his guilt dissipating. He might tell the story in passing to the guys after work. *Turns out my father was some guy named Jimmy. A guy with a perfect heart and a messy truck.* And then, like Evie: *It's ridiculous.* He could hear himself saying it. *She did it on purpose.* The guys would chuckle and then move on to another topic of conversation. Now, he was smoothing out the folds in each note and arranging them into a pile. Maybe instead he'd share this story with Evie. His own collection of smooth stones and birch sticks in every crevice of the car. Just like his father. His heartbeat quickened, but Jim didn't feel his usual sense of doom. Maybe it was his mother's heart that he'd inherited, Jim thought. Despite everything else, hers had been strong. He pictured her through the hospital window, arms waving, the flying Kleenex turning to crumpled notes. Magic.

"Let's start on the bedroom," Evie said, shaking Jim's shoulder. "We'll treat ourselves to a coffee break when we're done." Jim's anger rose as he remembered her games of bribery from childhood. *Clean your room, Jimmy, and then we'll watch cartoons.* "This'll get faster, I promise."

Her control, her cajoling—she was always just trying to cheer him up. He suddenly understood his sister's need to take charge. He pictured the bittersweet taste of Nabob sweetened with honey, the way Mom had done it. The notes spread out before them, Jim telling his story at the old kitchen table, letting a small crack form in the wall he'd put around his heart. Out of the corner of his eye, he could almost see more notes poking out of dresser drawers and peeking from behind mirrors, rewriting his history. At the doorway, Jim steadied himself and stepped forward.

BONES

E. J. Nash

The skeleton in my closet is loud tonight. She doesn't make it very easy to sleep. Her bones *click-clank-clunk*, porcelain-white, grinding a few feet away from my bed.

"Are you having trouble sleeping?" the skeleton asks. Her voice is muffled from behind the closet door.

"Yes," I admit.

"Good," she says.

I am a little spiteful, so I've made my closet as uncomfortable as possible for her. Like geological strata, there are layers to the detritus. First come my shoes, from these-will-kill-me heels to heavy winter boots to Converse to flip-flops to my work boots that Jackie once called "badass." Old sports gear is next, archaeological artifacts from younger years: tennis rackets, a basketball, golf gloves, shin guards. Last was my "stuff" layer, a mishmash of shirts and board games and paperback novels I said I would read and never did.

On top of it all, the skeleton lounged.

"Whatcha thinking about?" the skeleton asks now.

"Sleep," I said.

The alarm clock on my bedside table screams that it's three in the morning. I have a lovely vision of throwing it out the window.

"I don't think you should sleep."

"Not surprising."

"I can surprise you."

"Please don't."

I haven't always had a skeleton in my closet. She appeared the day I heard about Jackie. I opened my closet, looking for a black dress, and there she was, eyeless and meatless and somehow staring right at me. Weeks later and my scream is still caught in my throat, red-hot and raw.

"I'm bored," the skeleton says. She raps on the inside of the closet door in a pattern. *Tap. Tattaptap. Tap.*

"There's a lot of books in there."

"I don't want to read."

"Want to let me sleep?"

"Not really."

Milky streetlight filters in through the blinds. My bedroom is small and untidy. One bed. One dresser. One chair.

And, notably, one closet.

"You should think about me," the skeleton says, just like she said yesterday, and the day before that.

"I don't want to," I mumble.

Her bones crunch and pop as she readjusts her position. "You were quite mean to me, you know."

"Thanks for the reminder."

"I'm glad to be helpful."

Jackie had been so withdrawn. Cancelling plans. Not showing up. Snapping at me, her friend from college.

I snapped back.

I don't want to be friends anymore, I'd said, immediately regretting it, but it was like spreading salt over soil. Poison the earth, kill what grows.

Some things you can't take back.

"Sticks and stones—" the skeleton starts to sing, and I cut her off.

"I didn't call you any names," I said.

"Taking back a name hurts more," she says, and the name is *friend*.

For the first time, the closet door creaks open.

"What are you doing?" I catapult back against the headboard. Panic spikes through me. My lamp is on the bedside table. It's too far away to turn on. I am petrified, turned to stone as the closet door slowly swings outward. Streetlight catches a sliver of her as she slinks through the door and stands next to my bed.

"Hello," she says.

I've never seen her outside of the closet. Vertebrae like

razors, fingers like needles. Her eye sockets are empty holes.

She climbs onto the bed and crawls toward me.

"Why now?" I manage to rasp. Of all the nights, why tonight?

The skeleton looms over me, holding one of those needle fingers above my mouth, tracing a line over my lip, and I can see the future. She will stick the finger down my throat, gag me, choke me, open me up, slip inside, replace my bones with hers. Calcify me from the inside out.

"It's the day we met," the skeleton says, tapping me on the forehead, and I remember Jackie walking up to me on the first day of class, Jackie with the night-black hair, Jackie with the smile, Jackie from two years ago, Jackie before the cancer ate her bones.

"I didn't know," I whisper. "I'm sorry. I'm so sorry."

She hadn't told anyone about her diagnosis. I didn't know she was sick until she died. Until I'd already hurled those words at her.

I don't want to be friends anymore.

The skeleton edges closer. Looks at me. I could fight her, kick her, slap her, stab her, fear her. I could live with her in my closet. But she won't stay there.

The skeleton jams one bony finger into my mouth. I instinctively recoil and spit out the ashy taste.

Then I lean forward and capture the skeleton in an embrace.

"What are you doing?" the skeleton asks, and her words vibrate underneath my hands.

"I'm sorry," I tell her. "I'm so sorry."

The night is soft. Gentle. Quiet enough that I hear each bone shift as the skeleton hugs me back.

"Do you miss me?" she asks.

"More than anything."

By the time my clock whispers that it's five in the morning, the skeleton is gone. Dissolved through my fingers. Dawn is a purple bruise at my window.

I lurch out of bed and stumble towards the closet.

Clothes. Books. Sports gear.

"Jackie?" I ask. I dig like a dog, throwing out the shoes and books and sweaters and she's not there, she's not hiding, she's gone, and that's the problem, I didn't know I needed the skeleton until she left.

I want her back.

I check under the bed, behind the curtains, in the bathtub. She's not there and that's worse, to be forgotten instead of hated.

"I hate you, Jackie," I say. The lie is bitter between my teeth. "I meant what I said. I don't want to be friends anymore."

I need guilt like I need oxygen. I'd rather feel bad than nothing at all. I'd rather have a splinter of Jackie than to have her disappear. I'd rather stay awake than sleep.

So I slip into bed. Feel the coolness of the sheets. The warmth of the duvet. "We were never friends at all," I say.

From the closet, I hear the shifting of bones, and I finally breathe.

SLIPPERY SILVER

Andrea Marcelino

There within her open hands laid the invitation. Her name written in perfect cursive. "Celeste, you are invited." The gathering would take place just after Christmas. The location was north of the city, where expanses of farmland had been converted into private property developments. An internet search revealed the satellite view of a very large house. It was never clear who among them was the host as no one presented themselves as such, and so the host remained nebulous and no one questioned it further. The curated guest list brought together twenty individuals, sometimes more, sometimes less, of unique qualities and tastes. The address was always somewhere different—a labyrinthine cellar, a musky dance hall, a dressing chamber in an abandoned theatre. She turned the invitation over in her hand, felt the weight and quality of the paper, and delighted in the colour of its text: silver.

She had once written a little poem about the moon that was published in a bi-annual feminist literary magazine and then, one day soon after, her first invitation addressed to "the poet" appeared in her mailbox, the elegant cursive in silver ink as if the moon herself had sent her approval. Celeste made a practice of preparing short verses to recite, no more than twenty lines, in the event someone would look around the room and ask, "Who can orate a poem from memory?" and she could rise to the occasion and play to their ears, upholding her rightful place among them. Now with invitation in hand, the flash of silver striking her pupils, she was stuck by an eagerness that she had not felt in some time. And a fear. What if they asked her questions? "What did you do with all your time, Celeste?" She was not a confident liar.

The last gathering had been three years ago. They could not say they were friends. The mystery of their separate lives kept them hungry for these reunions, wherein they could be whatever version of themselves they preferred, authentic or otherwise. She sometimes wondered what the other guests were like in their respective homes. Were they meticulous cooks? Were they generous lovers? Did they ever melt under the weight of a warm blanket? It was a curious exercise attributing everyday mundanity to this group because they seemed to exist outside of it, outside of dentist appointments and grocery lists and parking tickets; as if their real existences were extraterrestrial, beaming down to Earth for one night only to perform their best human.

On the night of the gathering, it was snowing. The roads were terrible and worse were the drivers juddering over the unplowed pavement. The 'For Sale' sign at the front gate and the absence of residential light confused the driver. "Are you sure?" he asked. The car cruised down the dark, private drive, lit only by the light of the full moon until they finally reached the large front door flanked by four thick columns like sentries guarding years of illicit secrets. Up close, a distant glow warmed the front windows like light seen through the smudged glass door of an oven. She opened and walked through the unlocked door and followed the hum of voices.

Didier was the first person she noticed in the front room. She almost didn't recognize him—his gaze blocked by a pair of large, dark sunglasses, and his striking ensemble too loud for a quiet corner, and yet, there was a familiarity she registered: his distinctive height, his impeccable posture, the elegant way he turned his head toward her when he sensed her eyes. He smiled at her and lifted his glass.

"I've decided to challenge every social norm and practice. It first started as an experiment but grew into a much more fruitful and extensive life choice."

"Very post-modern of you. What have you experimented with?"

"First with personal hygiene."

"You live alone, yes?"

"Yes." Then, he recited his list. "None of them lasted very long, except for clothing, obviously."

She studied his outfit now given clear permission to fully take it in—a green army surplus field jacket worn over a scuba wet suit, accessorized with a fur scarf wrapped tightly around his neck, and dark sunglasses. She smiled.

"Weren't you doing a... PhD in...?"

"In the Philosophy of Technology."

"Right, machines having feelings!"

"Reductively, sure. I've extended my research to any physical object created by humans, with a specialization in attire."

"Clothing with feelings then?"

"I'm working with an energy worker. We find pieces that hold a lot of energy, sometimes reconstructing them to emit specific vibrational energy waves when you wear them. It's energy curation essentially."

"So you're a stylist?"

"I work in energy, not style," he retorted.

"So vintage clothing but with crystals in the pockets?"

"No, not like that," he said. "This is much more powerful because you are wearing the energy on your skin. The organ absorbs it and then, you embody the energy."

"I see," she nodded.

"I'm currently wearing a curation of different protection energies... to avoid any contamination." He gave a slight, coy smile and arched a dyed-orange eyebrow above the frame of his sunglasses. She smiled in delight.

"I wonder what you would suggest for me," she said playfully.

He was silent for a moment, then, in a serious and considerate tone, said, "That would be difficult."

"Oh, I was just joking," she smiled apologetically as if she had given a secret part of herself away. She felt Didier's stare beyond his shades and was suddenly conscious of her own outfit. She wore a simple, long black dress that balanced comfort and formality. Her intention was to appear unassuming so as not to invite any prolonged looks. Rather, she had hoped for sights she could feast on and Didier did not disappoint. Yet, his wordless stare made her question if her choice was, in fact, all that inconspicuous. Breaking the silence, she said, "Well, if you do think of something, I'd be curious," she let her voice trail off and then excused herself to refill her glass.

At the bar, she encountered Faune, the science fiction writer. Faune explained that since their last meeting, she had taken up writing fan fiction of medical case studies featured in medical journals, which led to the unfortunate circumstances of people believing her work to be true. She had since given multiple public talks in an attempt to convince the people that her writings were works of fiction, but by then, new claims were made that she hadn't written them in the first place.

"It's been a real mess, but I've met some really interesting people."

"I'll bet."

"And what have you been up to?"

She had prepared for this question, but every lie she practiced in the mirror came out too thin. The truth was not for this crowd. How could she tell them that she had spent most of her time abandoning her creative and professional pursuits for that of homely ambitions? For stability and mundanity, subjugating herself to household routines, and yet, up until that point, it was all still in vain. Nonetheless, she needed to deliver some kind of answer and now was the time to recite the precise string of words she had settled on and hope for the best:

"Not much. I did a variety of psychedelics and mentally travelled to distant galaxies, and when I came back, I recreated and recorded the sounds I had heard on my astral journeys."

"I thought you wrote poetry?"

"I do, but poetry and music are very closely related, you know, rhythm, patterns, sounds. I've expanded my creative energy field."

"How wonderful." Faune smiled and then picked a loose thread off the cuff of her olive green pantsuit.

"You know, that reminds me of a story I've written," Faune began, but was soon interrupted by Annabelle's sudden appearance at her side.

The sight of Annabelle was always a mixed welcome. She could be interesting and exhausting in the same breath, propping herself up as morally superior in any conversation, and so a cordial exchange meant agreeing with everything she said. Her life was a tightly wound string of mysteries and inconsistencies, loosened and further confused by casual reveals—she had squatted in an artist commune in Berlin; ran a dog shelter in Vietnam; once chained herself to an old-growth tree; met the Dalai Llama; had an ASMR YouTube channel; produced homemade vodka. She had a number of vocations and did not identity as one thing. She was now a Professor of Something.

She had grown out her bangs which now hung like curtains over her eyes.

"How do you see under them?" Faune asked.

"At first, I wanted to see less, but then my eyes adjusted and now they see everything again." She carefully lifted her bangs from her forehead and revealed a third eye. "Then this grew and now I see things unseen."

Celeste and Faune stared at it—unlike Annabelle's other two eyes, which were dressed in heavy liner and mascara, this one was naked and bare, just a pale blue eye under a soft and creamy lid.

"Can you see the future?" Faune asked excitedly.

"No," Annabelle said placidly. "I see the energy around each person. I see infinite potentialities."

"Can you see other timelines?" Faune asked.

"Almost," Annabelle replied.

Annabelle's milky third eye blinked slowly and a translucent liquid, thicker than tears and almost sparkling, seeped from both corners of the eye, enthralling Celeste. The eye shifted its focus onto her. It made her twitch and feel a strange pressure in her stomach. Then, Annabelle swept her bangs back over her forehead, covering the eye.

"It's exhausting, to be honest," Annabelle said.

"You seem relaxed," Faune replied.

"That's the CBD oil." She smiled. "I make my own now, the industrial stuff is terrible. I put mine in every drink."

A bell rang. *Finally*, Celeste thought. The sound marked the main event, the very reason for their attendance—a culminating spectacle to delight the senses and satiate their creative appetites for inspiration. Every gathering had one and each more extraordinary than the last. She still dreamt of the gathering where she had witnessed a dead bird come back to life.

A young man Celeste didn't recognize said, "Please move to the third room."

Celeste hadn't been counting rooms, but she followed the shuffle of people to a large, adjacent one. It was unfurnished beyond a singular wooden chair.

"Please move back. Do not the block the chair." He spoke in such complete sentences, one could almost hear the period.

The unrehearsed crowd moved further into the room, giving an unobstructed view of the chair. It was the first time since arriving that Celeste took full notice of the assembled group now all tightly huddled together. Her heart swelled to be once again among them.

"We have a special guest here tonight. She finally accepted our invitation," the young man said with a final courteous smile and left the room.

A distant gong was struck and the room went dark, save for the light from the full moon that came through the large window and shone a perfect spotlight on the positioned chair. They all watched the chair and a thick silence settled over the room. As the time passed and the stillness remained, Celeste grew anxious. What was she supposed to be doing? She scanned the other guests for clues. She noticed a slow but definite loosening in their faces as if their jaws were freed from a tight grip.

Then, a gasp sounded from one of the guests. Then, a distant yelp. Then, gradually, a wave of sound broke through the crowd as bodies shifted and clothing rustled. Celeste saw widened eyes around the room like fairy lights in the darkness. She looked back at the chair but it remained unchanged.

"Do you see her?" Annabelle whispered in Celeste's ear.

"No, I don't have a third eye," Celeste replied.

"No, with your regular eyes," Annabelle responded. Celeste felt a sinking sensation in her gut. She said nothing. She stared at the chair and its emptiness bore down on her. She knew what they saw. The wound was sharp, she almost tasted metal.

How many nights had she called for her? Too many to count, years worth now. She would pull back the curtains and let the moonlight shine on her bare belly, asking to be full like her, asking to illuminate what she was hoping to grow inside her. She had turned everything into a ritual as her offering. Tracking her cycles, rubbing her belly, making the necessary appointments, taking the necessary medication, and then, at designated times, laying supine on the examination table, feet on the footrests, splayed and ready for medical intervention as they slipped the silver inside of her. She imagined her belly protruding and a beautiful fullness that comes from being tethered to the earth.

But month after month, her own moons, unplanted, disintegrated and exited her body. It was a longing that took over her life. She couldn't remember the last time she had written a decent poem. She felt she had forgotten all the good words. No one could give her a definitive explanation but they continued to book her new appointments and she continued to carry out her rituals, but with a deepened wrinkle between her brows. Everywhere she looked reminded her of what she was still denied, and the years were passing.

The empty chair was yet another reminder. Tears cascaded down her face, she could almost hear the rush of water. Annabelle grabbed her hand and squeezed it.

Brightness returned to the room, revealing the elated faces of the guests.

"What a vision!" someone said.

"Unforgettable," said another.

Faune approached Celeste and Annabelle. "It was like something right out of my books! Have you ever had such a remarkably transcendental experience before?"

"Yes," said Annabelle.

Faune noticing Celeste's tears, "I was on the verge of tears too!"

"Yes, it was extraordinary," Celeste quietly replied.

The gathering was then over and they made their way to the front entrance. They all vowed to return with renewed commitment and said their genial goodbyes.

Celeste arrived home to her quiet, one bedroom apartment, tired and depleted. She didn't care to remove her makeup or brush her teeth or carry out any nighttime routine. She undressed and let everything fall to the floor. But she drew back the curtains to see her. She didn't ask for anything this time. She looked up at her lucent completeness, said goodnight, and went to sleep.

The dream came shortly after. Celeste was in the same large room with the same wooden chair. Again, the moonlight came through the window to form a perfect spotlight on the single chair. Celeste was alone this time. She felt the water rise up in her eyes as she stared at the barren seat. All of a sudden, Annabelle appeared, grabbed her hand, squeezed it, and said, "Soon."

OVOMANCY

K. R. Wilson

This is what the egg tells me.

Today Marcel will go to lunch at a bistro near his office. He'll leave his desk and walk down the cream-coloured corridor, noticing the scrape Brett's belt buckle made on the wall when Tess hammerlocked him into it after another unsubtle innuendo. He'll fleetingly miss Tess, who was relocated to another building after a confidential HR process. Brett—like Marcel, a lawyer—will still be there. Tess will not. Times two. Not a lawyer. Not still there.

Marcel's walk will take longer because of his foot. Two weekends earlier, a half-buried shell at a lake north of the city will have sliced it mid-sole, requiring three stitches at a regional hospital. He'll be using the cane he bought when he sprained his knee two summers before that, when he figured out that a cane works better opposite the injured leg, not next to it. His cane will tick on the hardwood of the elevator lobby, its rubber foot-cap having worn through along its edge. He will remind himself to stop at the drugstore on his way back for a replacement. The glass circle of the elevator button will light up at his touch with the whiteness of a soft-boiled egg.

Two blocks from his building, along the street frontage of a construction site, he will pass through a scaffolded side-walk canopy of rough planks strung with light bulbs in wire cages. The site's entry gate will be littered with debris from its trucks. Gravel. Bits of concrete. A half-block farther along will be a low-rise heritage building with hot yoga studios and interior design offices and, taking up the length of its ground floor, Uovo Magico, its patio marked off by geranium-filled planters.

As Marcel approaches the hostess podium, two young men with rolled white sleeves and jewel-toned silk ties will cut around him and his cane and tell the tattooed hostess they want a table on the patio. They won't have a reservation. The hostess will tell them the patio is full. One will point to an empty table and ask *What about that one*? She'll point out the 'Reserved' card. He'll raise his Breitling wristwatch—it will be four minutes past noon—and suggest that if the reservation hasn't been claimed yet, the table should be fair game. But she'll hold her ground. They'll accept an indoor table, which she'll show them to. Near the kitchen. Their penalty.

When she returns, she'll tick Marcel's name from her reservation book, take two menus from the podium, and lead him through the interior and back out to the table the white shirts had wanted. Two place settings with white cloth napkins. Marcel will pick up the 'Reserved' sign and hand it to her with a smile. She'll smile back as she slips it into her apron.

As Marcel hooks his cane on the table-edge he'll see the foot-cap is now separated almost all the way around and will remind himself again to pick up a replacement. He'll unfold the menu, though he will already know what he wants. Something else might catch his eye. His favourite might have vanished. These things happen. The menu will emphasize egg dishes, many with contrived names. The Uovo Easy. The I Wanna Take You Eier. And Marcel's usual. *The Ovomancy?* his usual server, Larissa, will ask, having quietly threaded her way through the other tables.

Yes, thanks. And a Peroni.

With a glass, Larissa will say. A statement, not a question. *Yes, thanks,* Marcel will answer, as if it were.

She'll bring them on a cork-lined tray, condensation bright against the bottle's dark green. He'll watch her pour. Backlit by the sun, the beer will seem to generate an inner amber glow.

She won't take away the second place setting, or even ask. She'll know Marcel's standing ruse—a lunch companion running late—in case one of his more socially forceful co-workers passes and thinks to join him. These things happen.

His first sip will have the savour a sunny day brings to

beer. Especially after a cane-slowed walk. He'll take a second sip and save the rest for his meal. This will be the best moment of his day so far. He'll bask in it.

As he does, he'll hear the growl of an overpowered car from the street to his left. He'll turn to look, with the veldt-born human sensitivity to growls. In this case, from Brett's bruise-purple Corvette. The recent one that looks like someone tried to draw a Ferrari with an Etch A Sketch. Its windows will be down. It will stop fifteen lateral feet from Marcel's table. Brett will glance over. Their eyes will meet. Brett's manscaped face will look mildly surprised, and he'll smile. Not a warm smile. A smile of 'Well, isn't this an interesting development?' He'll notice the empty place setting. *D'ja get stood up?* he'll call out. Marcel's stomach will sink. *Hang tight*, Brett will say.

The traffic will move. With a fresh growl, the Corvette will jerk forward and then lurch to a stop just short of a grey Mercedes. It will occur to Marcel that for Brett, the point of the Corvette won't be its horsepower—which is getting the better of him—but simply its bare, purple-y Corvettiness. Marcel won't own a car, but he'll be confident that if he owned a Corvette—as unlikely as his getting his face manscaped—he'd look into courses to help him master it. Precisely what Brett wouldn't do.

Just beyond the construction gate a burgundy Audi will pull away from the curb. Brett will give Marcel a thumbs up. Surely someone else will take it, Marcel will think. But no one will. It will take Brett six back-and-forth maneuvers to park. As he walks back to the restaurant he'll scan the patio for a direct opening that isn't there. He'll make a sweeping gesture to show that he'll come through the restaurant. The hostess will lift a restraining hand as he passes, but he'll be moving with such confidence she won't make a further effort to stop him.

Dude, he'll say loudly as he comes out to Marcel's table. The facing chair will make a harsh scraping noise against the concrete as he pulls it out, as if it's protesting the invasion of Marcel's space. He'll flop into it, knees apart. *Your lunch date a no show?*

There's still time, Marcel will reply. On the off chance it's not too late to discourage him.

D'ja get a text or anything?

Marcel will consider lying, which he'd be comfortable doing. The initial lie about there being a lunch companion is already out there. But Brett might insist on staying until the companion arrives, which could explode the whole ruse. *No, nothing*, Marcel will say.

Asshole, Brett will say. *Someone from the office?*

Friend from law school. She practices up north. Marcel actually does have a friend from law school who practices up north, so he'll have specifics to continue with if he needs them. *Must've gotten held up on the highway,* he'll say.

Larissa will arrive with Marcel's lunch. She'll hesitate at Brett's presence and give Marcel an inquiring glance. He'll respond by tilting his head a fraction in reassurance. A tiny exchange that will say all that needs to be said. Which Brett will be oblivious to.

Can I get you anything? Larissa will ask Brett as she sets Marcel's plate down. *What's on tap, darlin'?* he'll ask, draping his arm across the back of his chair, too animated for the metaphorical room if he'd bothered to read it. Which he wouldn't. She'll start reciting Uovo's draught list. Eight items in, he'll order the first one. He'll stare at her backside as she leaves. *Wouldn't mind running barefoot through an acre of those*, he'll say to Marcel.

Marcel is confident that Brett's Myers-Briggs chart would show hard extrovert. Unlike his own. Not that Brett would submit to Meyers-Briggs. Or know what it was. Marcel likes to think he'd assume it was a Niagara Winery. Which is probably unfair to Brett, but amusing. *Mind if I start?* Marcel will ask.

Go wild. Brett will gesture benevolently toward Marcel's plate. His eyes will narrow. *What* is *that, anyhow?*

In a rustic bowl at the centre of a bed of rice and roasted vegetables will be two hard boiled eggs, their shells dyed a rich red. *The Ovomancy*, Marcel will reply.

The what?

Ovomancy. Divination using eggs.

Divination like, what, fortune telling? Brett will laugh. *Your lunch tells the future?* Marcel won't give a straight answer. *Eggs are a common symbol of life and renewal,* he'll say. He'll lift one from the dish and tap it sharply on the edge of his plate. The shell will fracture with a delicate sound. He'll start to peel it.

How's it supposed to work? Brett will ask.

Marcel will hold up the half-peeled egg. *You see the red patterns on the white, where some of the dye went through? The idea is they have meanings, if you can read them. There's a blurb about it on the menu.*

What, like reading tea leaves?

Yeah. Like that. Marcel will examine the patterns. He usually doesn't. He doesn't believe in divination. He just likes the tactility of the dish. But he will feel he should illustrate the process he's describing. There will be a wavy line like the surface of a lake. Below it a tiny shell-like curve. Two weekends too late, he'll think. Remembering the taste of Tess's tongue. The water mirror-still except where it caressed their shoulders. The softness of her breasts against his chest. So unexpected. So tentative. Interrupted so suddenly by the shell slicing his foot.

He'll recall, as he did at the time, Freud's notion that there are no accidents. That the mind knows things. But how could any part of his mind have known the shell was there?

He'll finish peeling the egg. Watch the play of light against its surface. Just an egg and some dye. He'll take half of it in a bite and put the rest back in its bowl.

Larissa will return with Brett's beer and a menu. *Anything to eat?* she'll ask him.

Not that, he'll say, gesturing toward Marcel's plate. *Do you have, like, nachos, anything like that?*

The closest is probably the Set Me Frittata. It's topped with salsa and cheese.

That'll do. And could you bring some hot sauce? He'll watch her backside again as she walks away, though at least this time he won't comment.

Brett's lunch will have arrived by the time Marcel cracks the second egg.

What's it say? Brett will ask, mouth half full.

Marcel hadn't planned to check. *I don't know,* he'll say as he peels.

Brett will point with his fork. *That line there looks kind of like your walking stick.* Marcel will turn the egg. *Maybe,* he'll say. The tiny curve at the top will look a bit like his cane's handle. *I don't know what that dot below it could be, though,* he'll add. *Yeah, whatever. It's just a way of digging into your mind, right?* Brett will push egg and salsa onto his fork with his knife. *Like an ink blot test.* Marcel will give him a surprised look. *What?* Brett will say. *I did psych in undergrad.*

Larissa will bring separate bills without needing to ask. They'll settle up. Marcel will tip better than Brett. Neither of them will be aware of this.

Want a lift to the office? Brett will look at Marcel's cane. *I'm parked just down there.* A thumb gesture toward the purple Corvette. Forgetting that Marcel had seen him park.

Thanks, no. I like the walk. With the cane I'm fine. Brett will look slightly disappointed, so Marcel will add, *I'll walk with you as far as your car.*

The white shirts will leave the restaurant just behind them. One will flirt loudly with the hostess as they pass her podium. Marcel, not looking back, will picture her ignoring him. They'll make their way along the sidewalk. The construction gate will still be littered with debris. The shirts will be half a block back, discussing cryptocurrency.

Brett will turn toward his car. *Last chance for a lift,* he'll say. Marcel, turning his head to decline, won't see the concrete lump where he's about to place his injured foot.

When his sole connects with it, he'll instinctively lift his weight. Shifting it to his cane. On his opposite side. Next to Brett. Who will be stepping toward his car.

The worn rubber tip will give way. The exposed wood will slip on the gravelly pavement. The cane will shoot sideways. Marcel will topple after it, landing hard on his hip. The cane will slip between Brett's feet, tripping him. Throwing him face first against the fender of his car. He'll yelp. Twist away from the fender. Flop on his back beside Marcel. There will be an instant of silence.

The white shirts will laugh.

Christ! Brett will shout, putting a hand to his face.

I... Marcel will start to say. Then he'll stop. Piecing together what happened. Brett will look at his hand. No blood. *Christ!* he'll say again.

One of the shirts will reach to help him up. *Hey,* he'll say, still kind of laughing. *Don't blame this guy.* Nodding at Marcel.

Yeah, his buddy will add. *Total accident. Dude, why didn't you avoid that rock?*

This to Marcel. Who will turn and see the concrete lump.

The first shirt will have Brett up on his feet. Will peer at his face. *You're gonna have a shiner,* he'll say. *Otherwise you look fine.*

Brett will gently touch his cheekbone. Then his eye socket. Nothing will alarm him. *What the hell happened?* he'll ask.

The shirt will pick a black rubber dot from the ground. *Your buddy stepped on that rock, and then his stick slipped. This must've come off it*. He'll shrug. *These things happen.*

Brett will look down at Marcel. *Shit man,* he'll say. *Are you all right?*

I think so, Marcel will say, kind of vaguely. He won't exactly be in the moment. He'll be thinking about Tess. And a dot on an egg. And something Freud once said.

Sometimes the egg is very specific.

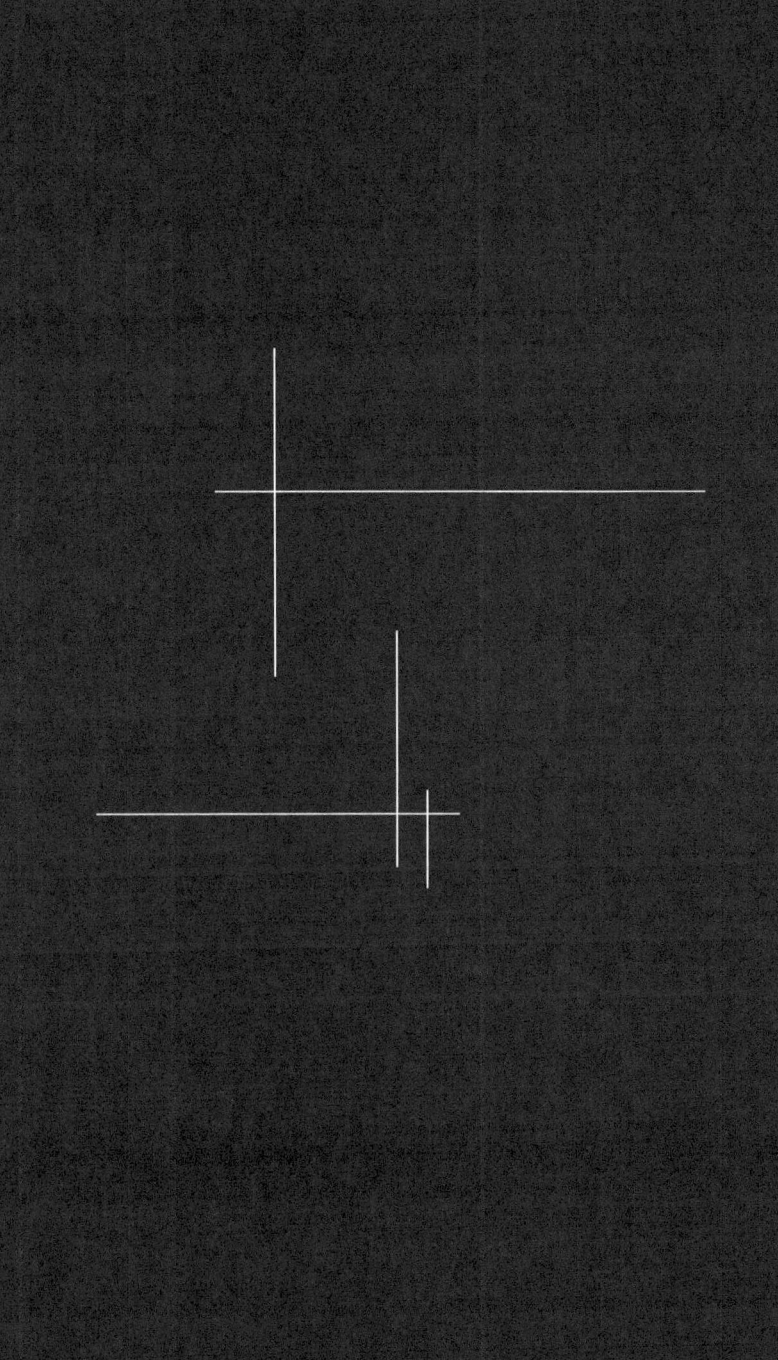

ABOUT THE AUTHORS

Nikki Berreth (pg. 29) is a writer of genre-bending fiction, a science communicator, and an informal educator from the heavily forested lands of Treaty 8 territory. Now living in the Pacific Northwest, she tries her best to impersonate a sea sponge by enjoying a simple life while soaking up all the knowledge and experiences that float her way. Unlike a sponge, she's a gifted storyteller and has performed her work for spoken word audiences, Science Slam events, and scientific conferences across North America. She s a collector of hobbies, and often enjoys mixing watercolours, cuddling her leonberger, and obsessing over her plants.

Rose Camara (pg. 13) is an emerging writer living on the Lekwungen people's territory/Victoria. Her work explores women's health, resilience, and agency. She's had pieces shortlisted in contests by *Room* magazine and *Flash Fiction Magazine*. Other than writing, Rose spends her time chauffeuring her children and transporting books to and from the library. Find her on Instagram @rosecamarawrites.

Andrea Marcelino (pg. 57) is an interdisciplinary artist born and based out of Tkaronto/Toronto, whose practice includes writing, photography, video, and film. She earned her MFA at EICAR in Paris, France and in 2019, was the recipient of a Canada Council of the Arts grant and a Toronto Arts Council grant for a short film project currently in post-production. Her main artistic focus is to tell impactful stories wth complex female characters, and demonstrate the importance of female storytelling in our narrative and visual culture.

Cornelia Mars (pg. 3) is a writer based north of Montreal. Her writing has been published in *The Capra Review, The Keeping Room*, and others, and is forthcoming in *The Humber Literary Review*. She holds a degree in English Literature and Creative Writing from Concordia University, and she was selected for the Quebec Writers' Federation's mentorship program in 2023.

E. J. Nash (pg. 51) is an Ottawa-based writer. She holds a bachelor's degree from The University of Western Ontario in Creative Writing and English Language & Literature, and a master's degree in Information Studies from McGill University. Previous work has been published by CBC, *The Globe and Mail, Nature*, and *Woman's World*. Two of her ten-minute plays, *Murder & Other Hobbies* and *Devil's Advocate*, were produced by Kanata Theatre. Say hi at ejnashwrites.com or on Bluesky @ejnash.bsky.social.

Katrine Raymond (pg. 39) is a mom and reading intervention coach living in Hamilton, Ontario. Her writing has been published in the *Theories of HER Anthology, Canadian Stories,* the *Dalhousie Review,* and *The Canadian Encyclopedia*. Her plays have featured in HamilTEN,

Supercrawl, The New Ideas Festival, the Toronto Fringe, and the Lamplighter Festival. She is grateful for the support of her family.

Tara Ross (pg. 19) is a writer, podcaster, and audiobook narrator based in Southern Ontario. She is Publisher's Way Coordinator for the Eden Mills Writers' Festival and co-hosts The Hope Prose Podcast. Her fiction and essays have appeared in *Tamarind*, *Dulcet*, and *Kaleidoscope*, among others. When she's not working as a Speech-Language Pathologist or being all things mom, Tara strives not to kill off wildlife with impossible odds of survival. Follow her writing journey on Instagram @tara.k.ross.

K. R. Wilson (pg. 69) is a Toronto-area writer. His novel, *An Idea About My Dead Uncle,* won the inaugural Guernica Prize in 2018, and his novel, *Call Me Stan: A Tragedy in Three Millennia,* was long-listed for the 2022 Leacock Medal. His follow-up novel, *Stan on Guard: A Two Part Invention,* will be published by Guernica Editions in 2026 and his SF-noir, *Tendrils,* by Palimpsest Press in 2027. His work has appeared in various literary journals and the flash fiction anthology, *This Will Only Take a Minutes*. He can be found at www.krwilson.ca and on social media at @krwbooks.

Other Canadian Short Story Anthologies
from Chicken House Press:

The Things We Leave Behind (2022)
Small Town Summer Nights (2023)
Will There Be a Sunset? (2024)